WITHDRAWN

minedition

North American edition published 2014 by
Michael Neugebauer Publishing Ltd. Hong Kong

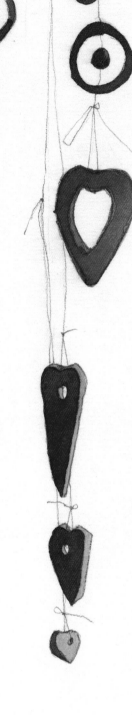

Michael Neugebauer Publishing Ltd., Unit 23, 7F, Kowloon Bay Industrial Centre,
15 Wang Hoi Road, Kowloon Bay, Hong Kong. Phone +852 2807 1711,
e-mail: info@minedition.com
This book was printed in January 2015 at L.Rex Printing Co Ltd 3/F., Blue Box
Factory Building, 25 Hing Wo Street, Tin Wan, Aberdeen, Hong Kong, China
Typesetting in Sabon
Color separation by Pixelstorm, Vienna
Library of Congress Cataloging-in-Publication Data available upon request.

ISBN 978-988-8240-92-0

10 9 8 7 6 5 4 3 2 1
First impression

For more information please visit our website: www.minedition.com

Catherine Leblanc

Here She Is!

Pictures by Eve Tharlet

English text adaptation by Kate Westerlund

minedition

Playing with Papa was one of Little Bear's favorite things to do. But Mama and Papa had told him that something special was going to happen.

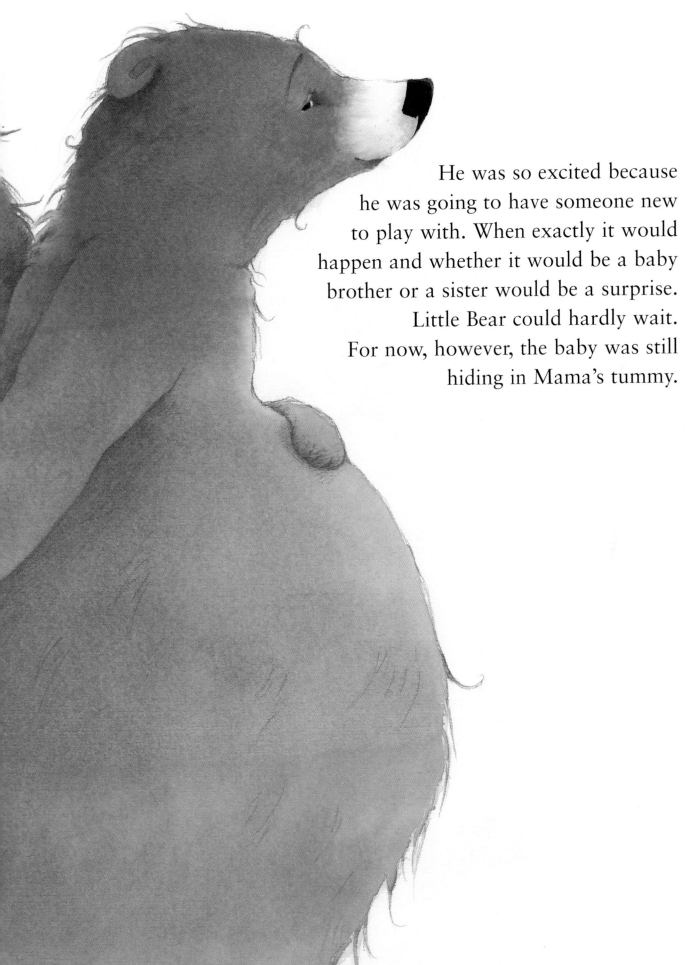

He was so excited because he was going to have someone new to play with. When exactly it would happen and whether it would be a baby brother or a sister would be a surprise. Little Bear could hardly wait. For now, however, the baby was still hiding in Mama's tummy.

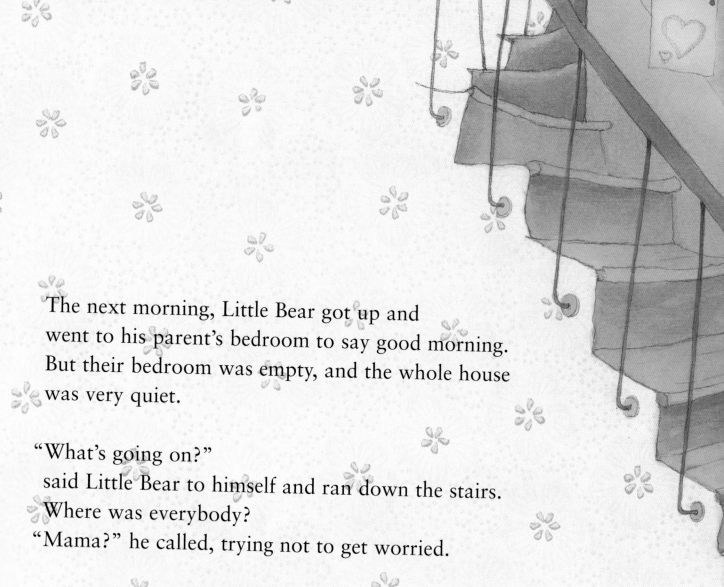

The next morning, Little Bear got up and
went to his parent's bedroom to say good morning.
But their bedroom was empty, and the whole house
was very quiet.

"What's going on?"
said Little Bear to himself and ran down the stairs.
Where was everybody?
"Mama?" he called, trying not to get worried.

To his surprise, his grandmother came out of the kitchen.

"Good morning sweetheart," she said. "Did you sleep well?"

"Where's Mama, where's Papa?" he said.

"Your parents are at the hospital. Your little sister was born last night.
Everyone is just fine, and this afternoon we will go and visit them."

Finally, the new little someone had arrived! Right away he began
thinking of all the things they could do together.

Little Bear found his mother holding his new baby sister.

"She's so tiny," he said.

His mother held the baby like a tiny treasure. That was his place, but he didn't say anything.

"Come closer and have a look!" said Papa.
"She's sleeping like a little angel. We want to call her Anna, what do you think?"

That didn't interest Little Bear one bit. He just wanted his place back, his place next to Mama. Slowly he made his way towards Anna. She didn't even open her eyes to say hello. He was disappointed and decided to play with Edward, his teddy, instead.

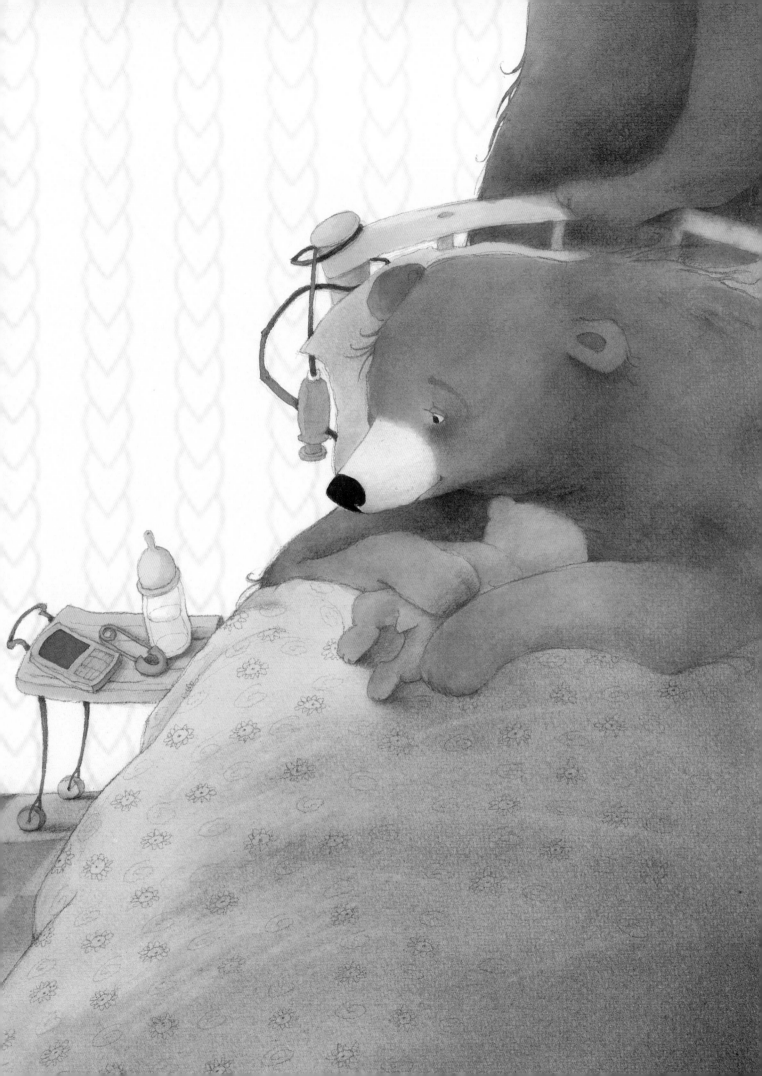

Soon they were all together at home. Anna was sleeping, and Little Bear got to play with his parents. It was great! Romping on the sofa, playing tickle games, but softly so they wouldn't wake Anna.
Little Bear thought how wonderful it was to have Mama and Papa all to himself.

But soon everything was different. Whenever Little Bear wanted to play with Mama, she was busy with Anna. Anna had to be bathed, Anna had to be dried, Anna had to be fed, and Anna had to be dressed.

"Sweetheart, you're a big boy now," said his mother, "and big boys can play by themselves."

He took his ball and went to find Papa.
"Will you come and play with me?"

"Not now, son, I have to help Mama."

And then he would hold Anna and say things like "Isn't she sweet"
and "She's so cute."

Little Bear did not understand it all. He was suddenly the big boy, and his mother and father only seemed to be interested in Anna. They always looked at her with such sparkly eyes.
"She can't even talk or walk by herself, and you can forget trying to play with her," he thought.

Now Anna was the one who got to sleep next to Mama or Papa. That had always been his place when he felt alone. Now it was just Anna, Anna, Anna…

She often cried or screamed loudly. Even worse, sometimes she was so stinky he had to hold his nose.
And his parents thought it was all wonderful.

Little Bear was no longer important.

"If they like stinky little bears," he thought, "then I won't wash, I can
  be stinky too!"
"What's the matter, Little Bear?" said his mother.
  He didn't say a word.

He went straight to his room and threw himself on the floor.
Then just as suddenly he jumped up and kicked his tower,
sending building blocks in every direction.

Then he had an idea. He took his teddy, Edward,
and lay down next to Anna on the play-mat.
He wanted to stay all day.
Anna just gurgled and cooed.
"We can't really do anything," he thought.
"She can't even play with her own rattle!
What do Mama and Papa find so great about her?"
he wondered.

Then he looked closer. She turned her head to him and looked at him with her great, big eyes. Her head seemed tiny, but it was round and soft. He gently stroked her cheek. "Her fur is so soft," he thought, "and she isn't really that stinky."

"Hello Anna," said Little Bear, "I'm your big brother."

Little Bear thought he saw a little smile on Anna's face.

With her wiggly little legs, she kicked him softly. Her legs really were little. He measured his paw against Anna's. It was much smaller than his.

He tried talking baby-talk to her, "Gurgle, gurgle, goo, goo."

She puckered up her little mouth to imitate him. Little Bear laughed, and Anna made baby-giggles. This was the first thing they had done together.

"But Anna can't do anything by herself," he thought.

"I know!" he said, "I'll build a castle with my blocks–for my little princess Anna!"

Then he asked, "May I hold Anna?"

"If you're very careful," his mother said as she gently put his little sister in his arms.

She was heavier than he thought.

Little Bear carried his new little sister to his room. He felt strong. It was time to show her his toys and to introduce her to his stuffed animal friends.

"Look, everyone!" he said.
"We now have a little sister, here she is!"

His mother looked at her two children.
She was so proud and happy.
"My big boy and my baby girl," she said.

Papa came in carrying the ball, "What do you think, son, do you have time to play with me?"

"Not now, Papa, don't you see,
I'm busy with my baby sister."